Psycho Babble and
The Consternations of Life

Psycho Babble and
The Consternations of Life

Richard M. Grove

First Edition

Panegyric Press
36 Second Avenue
Trenton, Ontario
Canada, K8V 5M6
pdroy@sympatico.ca

Copyright © 2008 Book - Richard M. Grove

All rights for story revert to the author. All rights for book, layout and design remain with Hidden Brook Press. No part of this book may be reproduced except by a reviewer who may quote brief passages in a review. The use of any part of this publication reproduced, transmitted in any form or by any means, electronic, mechanical, photocopied, recorded or otherwise stored in a retrieval system without prior written consent of the publisher is an infringement of the copyright law.

Psycho Babble and The Consternations of Life
by Richard M. Grove

Layout and Design – Richard M. Grove
Cover Design – Richard M. Grove
Cover Photograph – Richard M. Grove
Editor – R.D. Roy

Printed and bound in USA

Library and Archives Canada Cataloguing in Publication

Grove, Richard M. (Richard Marvin), 1953-
Psycho Babble and the Consternations of Life

Short stories.
ISBN 978-0-9732522-2-4

I. Title.

PS8563.R75F35 2007 C813'.54 C2007-902449-1

for kim
for her patience
for your love

thank you Doogla for . . .
   well, you know what for

Preface:

Here I am sitting in Martha and Rubén's Caribbean garden of paradise in Holguín, Cuba writing this preface. I have just finished editing this volume of short stories with the squeal of a pig and the cluck of chickens flapping in the background. I left the paradise of home in Presqu'ile Provincial Park, Brighton, Ontario, Canada to be here in this, my second home – Cuba, my second paradise, to work – if the word work could aptly describe the stimulating process of editing and writing.

There have been times of psycho babble and times of consternation in my life, most self inflicted, but now and for many years there has been little of either. I thank God for my surviving til now. I am grateful for this continued journey that has taken me to this place of relative harmony. The only bit of sadness involved with this Cuban trip is that my darling wife, Kim, could not be with me. She is a freelance writer and had some projects that made her reluctantly unable to join me for this last-minute adventure.

Psycho Babble and The Consternations of Life was born, primarily, out of three stories; *The Consternations of Will Farnaby, The Inner Voice, and H-E-Double Hockey Sticks*. Other stories and poems lent themselves to the theme of inner struggle and the cycles of life so were included, not just to make the book longer but to flesh out the theses and help round out this collection.

The Consternations of Will Farnaby, started off as a collection of unlinked short stories about different characters – some closer to life than others. Eventually they were put into an order with Bob as the main character linking them all together and then, for fun, I turned Bob into Will Farnaby after reading Huxley's "Island" - *See author notes at the end of the book.* These stories are purposefully dry and sometimes mundane in the depth of difficulties that Will Farnaby faces. These stories, like others are undoubtedly biographical on some level; how can they not be?

The Inner Voice, was a struggle for me to write until I found the vehicle to carry the thesis of spiritual growth – the journey. After studying metaphysics, meditation, Tai Che and very specifically Christian Science for most of my life this short story came to life. Much had to be edited out and rewritten before my biggest fear with this story, the fear of proselytizing, was overcome. My journey need not be the same for anyone else. I am still on my journey as you are still on yours, no matter how slow, fast, crooked or straight our paths might be. Am I the truck driver or Andy or a combination of both? It was only with the scrupulous editing from my friend, my editor and now my publisher, R.D. Roy, that this story is seeing the light of day. You will never see the editing notes that I ignored from him. You will never know if this story could have been better if I had followed all of his advice. I have been on the spiritual road of learning about my true spiritual nature for many years. Writing this story was part of that journey.

Finally *H-E-Double Hockey Sticks*, is for me, the third keystone to this book. First, do you know what the title means. It is an acronym for the word "Hell" – H-E-LL. The double hockey sticks being the double LL. "H-E-Double Hockey Sticks" was a slick way that a childhood friend's mother used to say the word – hell. I have heard it many times since and did not realize that everyone did not understand, its not-so-subtle, meaning. Follow the journey with this young lad and see if he thinks he will go to hell for stealing matches or not. In the end this short story has become the foundation for a short novel still in progress but still works fine in this original form.

All of the other stories and poems in this book including one of my favorites "The Glen Manor Inn" are about cycles of life, challenges and growth in some way or another. They are all fiction and simply part of my journey. I hope you enjoy them.

Contents

- The Glen Manor Inn – *p. 1*
- Micro Prose – Getting Married – *p. 9*
- Poem – Antonio's Only Resting Place – *p. 12*
- Micro Prose – Three for Three – *p. 13*
- Poem – Mario's Memories – *p. 15*
- H-E-Double Hockey Stick – *p. 17*
- Poem – Circumnavigation – *p. 24*
- Poem – The Chosen One – *p. 26*
- The Inner Voice – *p. 28*
- Poem – The Stifling Ruts of Discontent – *p. 36*
- Poem – Orbit of Violence – *p. 38*
- Poem – The More Things End – *p. 39*
- Poem – Koi in Perpetual Promenade – *p. 40*
- The Consternations of Will Farnaby
    - Aquarium Life – *p. 42*
    - The Walk Home – *p. 46*
    - Racoon Trappin' – *p. 49*
    - Psycho Babble – *p. 51*
    - Cold Steel – *p. 56*
- Biographical Sketch of Author – *p. 60*
- Author's Notes – *p. 64*

The Glen Manor Inn

NO ONE EVER KNEW WHY it went up in flames that night. It was a tinder box. For seventy five years this white frame inn baked in the sun, drying, creaking under its own weight. Uncle Bert used to say it was only a matter of time. Auntie Jen said it was God's way of punishing us for something we'd done wrong. "Search your soul, search your soul." she would tell my dad time after time. No matter how much we looked deep in ourselves none of us figured we had done anything that would provoke the wrath of God so much as to burn down a gem like Glen Manor. "God don't ever punish his children let alone by burning down a dream and putting people at risk! God wouldn't do such a thing." Mom would argue this over and over again but there was no changing Auntie Jen's mind on the matter.

Glen Manor came into our family back in the 1940s. I remember clear as a bell the time we all drove up to Killarney the first time to see her. Mom fell in love right off. She wandered round the twelve bedrooms muttering "She's perfect! Absolutely perfect!" Every room she entered she would say the same thing.

Dad was just a bit more practical with his feet planted firmly in the reality of how many broken windows needed to be replaced, how many floor boards were loose and how old the brittle cedar shingles were. "There is plenty of leaks in her Ma. The flashing round all four of the chimneys gotta be replaced an' the stone work round the north side chimney's gotta be knocked flat down and replaced right off. Couldn't build a fire in that fireplace 'til its done otherwise the whole place will go up in smoke. Lota work to get her in shape for payin' guests. Lota work!" he kept saying. Every room we went into, "Lota work."

Us kids didn't care about shingles, chimneys and such. We didn't even care so much about the lazy view that yawned its way up the hill from the sparkling lake. It was the dock and the row boat that drew us down the tamarac-lined lane to the cold red speckled rocks of the Cambrian shield. "The dock's got rot," Dad said "and the rowboat, not much point in doing anything to it. Drag it out of the water. We'll burn it soon as it's dry." Mom near flipped with joy. "We can buy it Pa? You sure Pa? I know it's a lot of work, Pa, but we can make a go of it. I know we can. You will see. Pa we'll make 'er right as rain in no time."

That was 1942. I turned ten that year. Dad was right about all the hard work it would take to get Glen Manor ready for paying guests. He drove us pretty hard but none of us ever complained because we had so much fun. That year I was the chief goffer. Go-for this and go-for that seemed to be my dad's mantra all summer. We never saw much of anyone all summer except for the trucks delivering lumber, nails, cement, paint, piping, wire and the list goes on. Dad wondered if it was going to make us broke before we had our first paying guest but sure as the last nail was driven into the new dock customers started to flock to our doors. Pretty soon we knew what real work was. Cooking, cleaning, hauling firewood, launching canoes and rowboats for customers and bringing them in again at night became just part of every day life summer after summer. For the next twenty years we never went home 'til after Labour Day and even then we went back up to Glen Manor every weekend till the ice on the lake froze over.

Year after year there seemed to be one adventurous mishap after another. Everything always seemed funny at the time. The seriousness never seemed to sink in until well after we laughed about it some. One year the Latton twins almost drowned trying to swim to the island. That wasn't funny at all until Dad reminded us that he pulled the twins out of the lake stark naked. You see, they figured that their swim suits were just going to slow them down some so they swam skinny figuring they would make it there and back without anyone knowing.

Another year Mrs. Smith, the fat old lady from Detroit, drove her brand new car down the hill and into the lake 'cause she pressed the gas instead of the brake. Her baby-blue wing-back Ford convertible made a mighty big splash as it dove off the granite cliff, out a sight, into the deep end of the point. We found her bobbin' like a cork. No, more like a floating pumpkin, screaming like a banshee, "Get me a tow truck to get my car out a the drink." I figured they would need the tow truck to pull her up the cliff first. I figured it was a good job it was a sunny day and she had the top down and could just float to the surface. I wouldn't have wanted to be the one to dive in to drag her out.

Yet another time old black Bart, we used to call him that 'cause of his dark tan and the black mood he seemed to drag around with himself where ever he went, rammed his pick up into the side of one of the lower cabins. He thought his wife was in there messin' with our gardener. Turned out it wasn't Clide she was messin' with but Jimmy our handy man. They both came screaming out of there butt naked. Covering their privates with their hands they ran straight down to the lake and jumped in. They stayed there until someone fetched them a towel and their cloths. We laughed about that for weeks after, in fact still do when we bring it to mind.

We had plenty of broken paddles at the dock, broken dishes in the restaurant and plenty of broken hearts down at Lover's Leap. Lover's Leap was just a high old rock looking over the lake with a mighty fine view. Despite these minor calamities we always managed to have fun but there was no calamity like the fire of "62 that burned Glen Manor to her stone foundation.

Dad figured Jimmy, our handy man wired a plug wrong under the new front desk. Dad was proud of that fancy counter and the new brass bell he bought so some one could ring it if they needed our help. The first time it got used was to wake everyone when the fire started. Smoke was already barreling up the wall with flames stretching for the ceiling before anyone knew what happened. There was no time for buckets, hoses or anything, just yelling and running to make sure everyone got out safe. Smoke billowed out of every window. Flames leaped over the eaves and up the cedar roof. Nothing could have stopped it. Dad was passing people out the side window, dangling them by their arms and dropping them onto a mattress he had just thrown to the ground. Kids were screaming, dogs were barking and then there was Mr. Kiles yelling frantically at me. "Save my money, save my money! I gave it to you in an envelope to put in your safe. There's $500 in that envelope and I hold you personally responsible. His face turned redder and redder as he screamed at me one more time to save his money. The thing was that we didn't have a safe so I simply filed it under "K" for Kiles or was it "M" for Mone?. At any rate it was on the top shelf just over the fancy new desk that Dad had built, where Jimmy had done the wiring and that is where the fire started and that was the last place I figured I was going.

Just as I arrived at the conclusion that it was not safe to go back into the house for an envelope of cash Mrs. Norman came running out of the front door. "If she wasn't burned, then you can go in to get my money," Mr. Kiles yelled. "Take her coat and put it over your head and get in there and save my money." Reluctantly I asked "Can I borrow your coat Mrs. Norman? I gotta go back in." With bashful timidity she looked over her shoulder in one direction and then in the other and with reluctance peeled the coat from her now naked body. Glowing a fine shade of pink in the aura of the blazing fire she dashed down the lane dodging from hedge to hedge looking for shelter for her goose bumped nudity.

With heroic effort and the image of Mrs. Norman's alabaster bum dashing down the lane, stored safely in memory, I dashed into the smoke filled lobby only to find Dad's counter being devoured in ravenous flames. There was no point in going even a step further. Turning to retreat I tripped over the shinny new counter bell. I stopped, stooped, grabbed it up and dashed back to the cool safety of the front lawn only to be met by Mr. Kile's belligerent demand to know why I had not retrieved his money. "You will pay, I swear," he bellowed as he huffed off like a child that had just lost his new ball.

"Is everyone out and safe?" called my harrowed mother."Where on earth is Mrs. Norman? Has anyone seen Mrs. Norman?" With a quiver of a smile I said I had seen her. "In fact more of her than she might like to admit. I'll find her and return her coat," I said as I turned and headed down the lane between flickering shadows.

The smoke took days to settle and weeks for my mother's nerves to calm. Glen Manor Inn was reduced to nothing but ash. Nothing but nothing could be saved let alone Mr. Kile's cash stuffed envelope. All that was left were the lower cabins, the boat house, dock and the precious view.

It took a few years but eventually Mom and Dad sold the land ashes and all. After all of these years even the old rotting rowboat, still under the tree melting into the ground was part of the deal.

Dad left the brass bell that I rescued sitting sadly on the granite front steps that led up into nothing but memories. Dad was sad but Mom was sadder still.

Gone were the days of Glen Manor and the fun times we had. Gone were the simple times of sitting watching the sun set. Gone were the creaky steps, the 100 year old grandfather clock, the oars over the fireplace used in the 1948 regatta when the Glen Manor team won first place. Gone was the register book listing every guest from every year and gone was the chest of photographs showing our annual picnics, dances and parties but never will be gone the memories of those precious times. It was simply time to move on as a new chapter of our life was about to unfold.

Getting Married

"I TOLD YOU WE SHOULD HAVE RENTED a limo to get married or at least taken a flippin' cab. This bus thing is for the birds. Now we're stuck in traffic and we'll never make it to the City Hall on time. Holy crap, look what time it is. I wonder what that says about us as a couple"

"Well, lets just be super negative here. Well maybe that's an omen. Well maybe we're just not supposed to make it. Well maybe we are just not supposed to get married. Holy crap is right. Lets just cut with the negativity."

"Negativity? Here I am sitting in a bus that is just crawling along, my hair is still wet, we are going to be late for our own wedding and you slam me with the negativity label."

"You should have gotten up earlier. If we don't make it on time it will be your fault."

"Now we are assigning blame are we? You wanted me to get up earlier? Go to hell. You were the one that wanted more nooky last night and then again in the morning."

"Oh, so it's my fault that you were so eager. Go to hell yourself. It's our wedding day damn it. If you didn't want sex you should have said so."

The bus inches a few more blocks. People are starting to turn and stare, or at the very least, surreptitiously peer at the couple's reflections in the window.

"We're never going to make it. Look at how slow we are going. Don't snuggle up to me and rub your nose on mine after you tell me to go to hell. Go to hell yourself. If I want an Eskimo kiss I'll whistle for Rexter. That's what you always do, flip out, tell me to go to hell and then you want to rub noses. What's with the rubbing noses thing anyway."

"Ok, ok, don't get all crappy on me. I know we are both up set but there's no need for a melt down."

"A melt down? What the..."

A mechanical voice spills into their fragile space causing them both to sit up and listen "Main Street, City Hall, transfer point to Bay Street"

"You see, I told you that we would make it."

"You didn't think we were going to make it any more than I did. Look we only have three minutes.

"I knew we were going to make it. You are the one that needs to learn to chill out."

The bus comes to a gentle stop, the doors hiss open and they bolt off like thoroughbreds out of the blocks. Grabbing each other's hands they dart through the crowd, bridge a toddler and hit the revolving doors at full gallop. "Which way is the bathroom. You go ahead. I gotta pee."

Antonio's Only Resting Place

THE SOUND OF HORSES, unhurried, echo outside the dark, still church. Iron rimmed wagon wheels rhythmically chatter over cobblestones drumming Antonio to sleep.

November can be a cruel time for the unemployed, the aged, with few warm places to relax, rest one's head to sneak ten minutes of grace.

These unforgiving oak pews have been polished with decades of waxing penance. Clutched by calloused fist they are his only resting place. These were the only doors open, the only warm place that offered him respite, reconciliation for the sins of being poor and old.

In the distance, shrouded with a heavy blanket of want, a lullaby of soft mutterings wash endlessly from curtained confessional. Please for absolution wafting through the heavy aroma of cheap candles. They are the tenuous scent of comfort. The trials of time melt, even if only for this moment, from his unshaven furrows of worry. Antonio rests.

Three for Three

"CAN I HAVE EVERYONE'S attention please. I would like to make an exchange. I can't giv'm away but would anyone like to trade. I got blue ones and green ones. Loads of both but that's it." Waving his arms in the air he raises his voice even louder. "Would anyone like to make an exchange?" The crowd stops their mulling and murmurs and turns to look his way. Heads perk up and people start to move towards the tall man in the shinny black suite. A voice bellows from the back of the room. "I've got some red ones mister. I've got too many of the damn things. Heck, I was just gunna smash'm against the wall for fun on the way out of here. I've got so many of 'm that I don't know what to do with 'm." He holds up a bag of ten or twelve gorgeous red ones. "They are the best you will ever see and they are fresh but I've got even more of 'm at home." The man in the black shinny suite gets down off of his wobbly chair and pushed his way through the crowd towards the man holding up the bag. "Trade ya three for three but I only need three." They make their exchange, shake hands and go off in their own directions smiling.

The man in the shinny black suit climbs back on to his wobbly chair and holds out his bags and hollers. "Anyone else? Anyone else wan'a make an exchange? What have you got there mister. What colour you got." The little man with a stubby beard, burried deep in the crowd, pushes forward and says. "I got a pocket full of little purple ones but they are hard and they ain't much use to no body. You want any of 'm, they are yours." The little man reaches deep into his pocket and pulls out a handful of the blackest purple ones you have ever seen. They are so hard they clink like marbles in his hand. "Sure pal. I'll take 'm three for three. What'a ya say. Three for three." The little man shrugs his shoulders and pushes forward. Three of my little purple ones for three of your blue? Sure any day. Sure you don't want more? I got lots." He starts to reach into his other pocket but the tall man in the shinny black suite turns his back on him and once atain returns to his wobbly chair.

"Come on folks, times runnin' out. If anyone has any others they are willing to exchange three for three then you gotta come forward now or it'll be to late. Three for three and I'll take any colour, any condition. Listen up everyone. Anyone else wan'a exchange three for three before it's too late?"

Mario's Memories

THERE IS NO POSSIBILITY that anyone will disturb the stillness of the backyard. No one has entered there for many months but still Grandpa Mario shuffles to the cedar gate and swings it hard. The sudden thud trips the deadbolt locked. He is once again utterly alone.

He mumbles his way slowly to the BBQ bringing it to life with the flick of a single match. "Would you like one burger or two my darling... only one?... One it is then."

He slips his grey stained apron over his head. It hangs loose, baggy, untied. It was a Father's Day present from his wife, too many years ago now to remember exactly when. Two frozen burger patties clink to the hot grill. Pershssss!

The gentle rhythm of the late afternoon spills in over the locked gate; splashing from the pool next door, birds chirping, distant traffic humming. "The children will be getting out of the pool soon and will be hungry. Should I put burgers on for them too darling... OK I will wait then."

Heat radiates from sun-baked, memory-stained patio slate. Cooking in silence Mario wanders through the landscape of his memories. The shadow hours of late afternoon have crept into his loneliness. It is this time of day that he is vulnerable to memories that leak into now.

H – E – Double Hockey Sticks

SUNLIGHT SLANTS THROUGH PERFECT, tiny, yellow leaves of a gigantic maple to cool virgin grass and outstretched legs. Clouds wander gracefully from the northeast over spring filled hills. Toe taps to a song that swims through mind like a leaf gliding on glistening ripples of a gentle creek. Life flows effortlessly, snaglessly to a sea unknown. It is early May.

"Mike, Mike, over here."

"Sorry I'm late, man. My Grams made me stack next winter's firewood against the wall of the back kitchen. I never stacked so much so fast and then she had me rake up the bark bits and then feed the rabbits. If it weren't a school day she would a' had me doin' something else and I never would a' made it. You been here long?"

"I've been here for hours. I snuck out before it got light. My Dad's up early so I figured I had better get up and feed the chickens before he gave me something more to do."

Mike kicked Chris' foot to make him move over to share the rock. He slid down and put his head on the rock and laid in the cool grass beside him. He toed off my shoes, no socks, and grumbled, "These are supposed to be my new shoes. Grams got them for free off a' one of her friends. Grams said I'll grow into them. Maybe by the time I'm twenty I figure and they'll be worn out by then."

"Mike, we are going to get in trouble for skippin" school. My sister wouldn't write us a note this time. She jabbered on about us going to "H – E – double hockey sticks" and she wasn't planning on joining us. She said she is going to tell Mr. Finlan that she has been writing all of those notes for us. She said she is going to go and confess to Father Horner as soon as she can make it to church so God doesn't punish her too."

"I might be goin' to hell man but not you. You've been going to church since you was born. My Grams never made me go. Not even once. Grams says there's no hope for me. I just try to stay out of trouble so as I don't get no beatin'. I figure hell's not worse than living with Grams, besides skippin" from school ain't goin' to get you into hell. You gotta murder someone or steal something big to go to hell. You don't go to hell for skippin" school."

Mike sat up and rubbed my sore feet. "Do you gotta wear shoes in hell. Maybe you just go naked, who knows. There's no girls in hell any way so who knows. The one good thing about goin' to hell is that Grams won't be there unless maybe there is a hell for women. Hell, I don't know. I guess no one knows for sure."

"I figure we just turn to worm food anyway so it doesn't matter much. My Mom has been taking my sister and me to church since forever but my Dad never goes. He says God is all around us and he doesn't need any church to pray. I figure Dad just doesn't like to shave till the afternoon on Sundays. I go just to make my Mom happy."

They laid there for a considerable length of time with their heads on that cold rock watching the clouds roll by and the sun climbing higher in the sky.

"Mike, what did you want to meet down here by the creek for any way and why did you want me to bring matches? I had to sneak them from the kitchen drawer." Chris laughed out loud and smacked Mike. He said, " I sure hope I don't go to hell for stealing penny matches."

Mike sat up and pulled a crumpled piece of paper out of his pocket. "This is why. You remember when I was over to your place a few weeks ago and we was watchin' TV and they was talking about fogivin' people and there was this lady that forgave a man who murdered her son and there was another who forgave this man for

rapin' her when she was just a little girl and she wrote him letters forgivin' him and she put them in the river and she said they washed out to the ocean and she was healed of grief and it made her life better? Well, I got to thinkin' about Grams and thought maybe I should write her a letter and put it in the creek only thing is that I want to turn it into a paper boat and set it on fire. We are too far from the ocean here so I figure I will put it up in smoke. If nothin' else it will be fun to watch.
    First I think I gotta read it out loud."

Dear Grams:

I'm sorry I wasn't particular tight with you when I was growin' up.
I am sorry that by the time I was ten you thought I was only worth hangin'.
I'm sorry that I had to live with you when Ma died and be in your way and all. Maybe if you had played with me, even just a little, when I was younger I might a' turned out more to your likin'.
I remember thinking that your house was like a train station, people comin' and goin' all the time. You hugged everyone that come through your front door. Every time you hugged someone and it wasn't me I hated you even more. Marylou used to hug me and make sure I had something to eat an'

she weren't even family. Even Bob, your repair guy, treated me good. He gave me a jackknife once and taught me how to skin a rabbit.

Do you remember that one time when Mr. Barker, gave me a cuff up the side of the head just for me bein' me? He made me cry right in front of you and what did you do? Nothin'!

Nothin' at all. You would have thought you might have at least pretended to care and give me a hug but you just gave me no mind and pushed me away as you walked off with that old Mr. Barker. I hated you for that and I hated Mr. Barker, the fat old bastard, even more. His pants were always hangin' low so as you could see his crack and he farted when he walked; I couldn't figure why you hung with him instead of me.

It wasn't till I was near fourteen, when I lost my boyhood to your friend, that old gal, what was her name? She had big boobs and a smile that made me shiver; I finally figured out you must have been runnin' a whore house. A whore house, for God sakes Grams, and Mr. Barker was your own personal customer. I sure hope that the old fart paid you good.

The TV says I gotta learn to forgive you Grams. Writin' ain't my thing so I'm not going to list all of the things that you done to me since Ma died. I forgive you for thinkin' I was dirt and just worth hangin' an' I forgive you for all that you done to me.

Mike

"Chris, show me how to make it into a paper boat. I'll put it in the creek and light it on fire and let it float away. What do you think?"

"I think you are nuts, man, but I know how to fold paper into boats, give it here. Me and my Dad used to take the Sunday comics after he read them to me and make boats and put them in the pond beside the barn. Here's the matches. Do you want to say anything more before you light it up?"

With silence a match was brought to life, the paper letter boat was lit by Mike and gently placed into the creek. Smoke streamed up for a flicker of eternity vanishing gracefully into the spring air without leaving a trace, ashes fell with a hiss into the creek's undulations. The ceremony was over almost before it started.

Circumnavigation

Through the stench caused by
fifty year old rolling steel
robbed of catalytic converters and filters,
air is filled with belching fumes
from low grade local petroleum.
We keep our heads down
as we trudge back to old Havana
fostering our human indifference
as if it were a precious commodity.
Squinting from heavy air
we breath with shallow breathes,
hunched avoiding toxic inhalation.

Heads down we stumble
on a sight that steers me,
involuntarily back.
Diverting awe struck
magnetized eyes,
I am repulsed yet drawn in for
rational explanation.
Mummified skeletal protrusions,
silently shrieks obscenities.
Matted petrified fur
and crushed scull,
tail still wagging free in breeze
as if greeting you

with bright eyes and slippers.
Demanding ponderance
turns to 10 second memorial,
once loved, petted, fawned over
now the mat of disregard.
Ignored by hundreds and hundreds
every day, month after month
now no longer seen as anything
not even as a sad lump of death.
This mummification is now
little more than a visual avoidance.
Sadder, head down,
mind back to dodging stench
we march on with stiffened apathy.

The Chosen One

Little do you know
that you are the chosen one
as you calmly chomp your way
from one green shady patch
under a giant Cedar tree to another
in the heat of a Cuban day.

You are the chosen one.
Round belly, soft velvet floppy ears,
a wisp of a grey beard that twitches
as you mindlessly stop and munch.

You are the chosen one.
Carefree, no concept of past or future.
Only one moment of now
strung into eternity.

You are the chosen one.
Hung by hind cloven hooves
to face dusty patch of red
stained earth,
left to sway gently.

You are the chosen one.
The pendulum of life
ticking
        life / death, life / death,
Paralyzed,
        motionless,

now still.
You are the chosen one.
Life drains from
your still pulsing neck
into dented tin pan
splashed to thin black pigs.
Hot life to squeals of delight.

You are the chosen one.
Not a single bray
will you utter in protest.
Not a single plea
or frantic flailing,
mesmerized by your duty
to succumb.

You are the chosen one.
Skinned, butchered, cooked,
served over a bountiful
bonding table of friendship.

You are the chosen one.
Your sacrifice fills the bellies
and the hearts of ten
with much left over.
You the chosen one
will live forever hanging
in this moment of gratitude.

The Inner Voice

ANDY NERVOUSLY SUCKED AIR IN and out through the gap of his front teeth. He tried to calm himself from the frustration that whirled through his mind like a blender on high speed. He remembered, his meditation teacher telling him, You get what you predict, you manifest, in your life only what is real and possible to you. Andy thought to himself, "I'm going to sit here and do nothing til I get a ride, I gotta get there and I'm going to get there and that is all there is to it."

The torrid sun beats down on his shoulders. Red dust from the parched fields billowed across the gravel parking lot, soughing over him like heavy smoke billowing off of a pile of smoldering leaves. Everything was covered in a wash of red. He squinted in the dry air, took a deep breath and ducked his head between his knees for shelter. Andy calmed for a moment before exhaling. Everything is a manifestation of thought, everything. There it is again, his teacher's voice looming, persistent.

With a slight lull in the breeze, he lifted his

head and gulped in another lung full of air. He mumbled to himself, "I'm going to get there but I just don't know how." Squinting he rocked back and forth, ducked his head and waited for what seemed to him the inevitability of a lull that would furnish the opportunity of another dustless breath. This is all that Andy knew, the breath was real, the spaces between breathes were real, holding his breath was real. Anything beyond breath was incomprehensible at this moment. Live in the harmony of now, all is well, came the voice again. If all he had to do was focus on his breath he felt he could cope while he waited for a ride.

"Hey buddy, you said you need a ride? I'm going north after all." A tall man with a red bandanna over his face waved to him to get into the truck. Both doors slammed shut, the din of dry wind quieted in the shelter of glass and steel. As the well-kept man pulled the bandanna from his face he said "Ralph, Ralph Watts from Middleton." He held out his hand to welcomed Andy into the dust free quiet. Flicking on the twang of country music the driver thumped at his chest and sputtered a cough. "Damn this dust cough, it's going to be the death of me yet. You said you are going north? How far?"

Without thinking much about it, words stumbled out of Andy. "If that is what you want."

"What are you saying? You are going north if I

want? Buddy a few minutes ago, before I went into the restaurant, I thought you asked if I was going north? I told you no but I got a call so now I have to see a customer north of here. Lady Luck is yours today. I'm going north all the way to..."

Without letting him finish, Andy interrupted. "If that's what you want. I mean your cough being the death of you. A guy once told me you manifest what you predict even for your body. You think your dust cough is going to be the death of you then sure enough if you keep knowing that as an inevitability then, sure as we are sitting here, it'll get you sooner or later."

"I don't reckon I know what your talking about but north it is." The driver thumped on his chest again, coughed and very gently, deliberately slow, pulled away form the truck-stop. "No point in making more dust than you have to. There is already enough to choke a rat. It is so hot and dry out there that your spit dries before it hits the ground. So how far north are you heading anyway."

Andy did not reply. He was off in his own thoughts mulling over what his meditation teacher had told him time and time again about living in the now.

The truck rumbled on for the longest time without either of them saying a word. For Andy the scenery dragged by like a black and white movie in slow motion. One still frame after another flashed before him; the haunting inner voice of his teacher persisted. You are not here by mistake, by coincidence or even by convenience. What did that mean – coincidence or convenience? There was something comforting about the idea of being in the right place at the right time but does that mean even now in this hell hole dust storm that I'm not here by mistake? That I'm in my right place, even right now?

The ideas he was taught came back to him in bits. He wondered what was the point of being in one place or another. The point is in the being. The point is living in the now. If the point is in the being then is it even possible for me to ever be in a wrong place? Andy hadn't quite figured all of that out yet. He was simply still struggling with the idea of living in the now and just what that really means.

The driver coughed again and thumped his chest, "This cough is going to be the death of me."

"If that is what you want," Andy said. "You predict it, you know it and you will manifest it sooner or later, one way or another. You can't help it man, that's just the way it is. Everything is a manifestation of thought, good or bad."

You sure are a perplexing fellow. First I find you sitting out in the dust storm with your head between your knees, I figured you had lost your marbles and needed help and here you are sitting in my truck telling me, that what I predict is going to come true and that I am going to die of a cough or some psycho babble like that. So what is it that you are trying to tell me and why?. If you start trying to sell me Jesus or anything like that then I predict one thing will come true for sure and that is that I'll pull over and let you out right here in the middle of no where. So where you going, if you don't mind me asking that is. I gotta let you out some where."

"Mister, I'm sorry, I don't mean to be rude, its just my teacher's voice that I keep hearing in my head. It keeps reminding me that everything has to do with what we think. I sat down in the dust storm beside the restaurant and figured, even in the middle of a choking dust storm, I'm in my right place even though I have to get home to my family and quick, I'm in my right place. Then sure enough you came along and told me you were going the wrong way to give me a ride. It is not like there is much of any traffic on this road. I just sat there and just knew I was going to get a ride from someone. How come you got turned around going north anyway? It was the Divine that's why. It doesn't have anything to do with a customer really. I keep hearing things over and over again. Everything is a manifestation of thought. We get what we predict, we predict what is real and possible to us even for our body. I tell you man, the voice comes from my teacher. I can hear him like he was standing right here. You are not here by mistake, by coincidence or even by convenience, my brother. You are here because the Divine wants you here. Right here, right now, living in the now is where you are supposed to be, my friend. What the heck am I doing in your truck in the middle of a miserable dust storm, hearing those ideas over and over again?

Andy rubbed his dusty hands over his face. "I can see how those ideas impact on me right at this minute but for you I figure the ideas I'm hearing are about you and your cough prediction. You keep saying your cough will be the death of you. Are you sure you want to hinge your idea of life to your dire prediction? Just for an experiment why not start changing the prediction to something positive?"

The driver turned to Andy and looked him up and down. "You kind a remind me of my son. He's studying at a university out of town in the geography department but he studies yoga and meditation and stuff like that on the side. He's got a head full of ideas like what you are trying to sell me. We've been driving for a while now. There's a truck stop coming up in about forty minutes. I'm gunna stop for a coffee and a pee. The driver coughed, thumped his chest and said, "I predict that I won't die of a dust cough before I get you to where you are going my friend. How is that for a prediction?"

The Stiffening Ruts of Discontent

The constant grumbling of discontent,
the snarls and huffs of judgement
are the utter and sad norm for him.
"Would you like a slice of meat?"
        eyebrows furrow
"I can see it's there.
If I want meat,
don't you worry,
I'll have meat."

There was no utterance
of a thank you.
Not even the thought,
not a spec of gratitude
seemed to cross his mind.
"I can reach it if I want it.
I can reach anything on the table."

He stabs at the cheese
that had been carefully,
almost decoratively laid out
on a small flower plate, bringing
three small pieces
to his slice of bread.

The shadow of silence settles
back in around the table
like oozing red mud,
instantly filling
the rut of a fresh tire track.
The heat of spring sun
will soon shrink
and bake the deep ruts
into unforgiving clods
that will not give way until
the love of cool rain.
Until then grass will grow up
around these red ruts, water will pool;
birds will drink and sing,
dip and flutter in ruts' shallow wells.

Orbit of Violence

You, like Io
in Jupiter's alluring embrace
revolve in orbit
around your captor.
One moment almost out of range
at furthest reaches of your journey
with his lessening pull on you
you are not quite ready to slip
from his magnetic charm.

The next moment pulled back
a moth to candle racing
into the arms of his singeing embrace.
Wings burned you are one of many moons
that revolve in yearning attraction
an appeal not worthy of your potential.

Will you ever realize that while in your
non-symmetrical elliptical orbit that you are
nearest your perfect self when furthest
his relentless gravity.

Will you ever realize that your violent
volcanic seething lessens only as you once again
spin to his outer reaches
once again almost out of grasp
only to spin to your endless cycle
of demise in time without end?

The More Things End

The earth goes round and round
The sun rises and then it falls
All will be the same in the morning
The more things end
The more we find ourselves at the start
The sun rises and then it falls
The clouds fill the lakes
The lakes the rivers
The rivers run forever in one direction
All will be the same in the morning
The more things end
The more we find ourselves at the start
As one breath leaves our body
One more is on its way in
The earth goes round and round
The sun rises and then it falls
All will be the same in the morning
The more things end
The more we find ourselves at the start
Never ending
Never starting
All will be the same
Until things change

Koi in Perpetual Promenade

Restaurant babbling bubbles float, glass beads of fragility skim under mirrored surface. Back and forth, forth and back, fancy gold koi, some silent black, some heavenly silver, glide in perpetual promenade. I don't have to talk to them and they don't have to listen, a perfect relationship of content banality, feeds me while I wait for my food. Forth and back, minutes turn to years, back and forth, gliding, caressing, careening off of each other, standing motionless facing corner, stuck mesmerized by silicone stripe of perfection, then back and forth, sucking gravel under queer, blue tinge of fading years. The limiting idea of a coffin shaped lake does not seem to bother them, placed in front of a broccoli green wall, stained with time, tunneling through months and years of ignoring bobbing plastic flowers with gorgeous red and white blooms of perfection. Back and forth, forth and back, forever waiting for a splash of food to break the monotony of forth and back. My food comes, cod not koi. Promenade continues.

The Consternations
of Will Farnaby

Aquarium Life

IT IS A BEAUTIFUL SUNNY, OCTOBER, day with a thin breeze. Will Farnaby and his good friend Frank sit in the only sunny corner of the almost deserted, patio bar. The whir of busy downtown traffic forced them to raise their voices from time to time.

"Oh man, you are always nattering at me about how I've gotta change my life. Don't bug me and tell me that I'm trapped in my little life and have to get out more. Everyone, including you – everyone – is trapped in their own little lives and besides I'm quite happy with who I am and where I'm at."

Will's face flushes after raising his voice above the traffic, which suddenly dropped off to quiet. He quickly lowers his pitch to match the lull. Leaning forward he pushes his face closer to Frank.

"Everyone, eventually stops fighting the inevitable barriers that hold them back and make them feel trapped. Even my stupid, little, goldfish stopped fighting the impermeable barriers of a glass wall. Sometimes I feel like the stupid thing is smarter than I am. He quickly stopped bumping into the walls of his aquarium and resigned himself to the box life of being fed and gawked at."

A cool grey laps at Will' back. The late afternoon has crept up and over his shoulder. He shuffles his chair a bit to the left, now more in the sun he continues, "All my life I have felt like I was a goldfish trapped in a gurgling aquarium. A long time ago I learned not to bump into my glass prison walls as I peered out into the expanse of my limited universe but nonetheless the barriers and limitations of life were there. I have always felt trapped in what seemed like an ever shrinking aquarium. Me peering out, everyone else peering in tapping on my glass wall wanting me to swim around and smile. Frank don't you ever get depressed with life and wonder why you bother sticking around? I have to admit to myself that as I shrank into myself everyone simply left me alone in my little coffin size cubical. Sure, sure, I know it is my own private little, safe, aquarium of my own making. I figure that as long as my inbox is cleared by the end of the day my tiny-minded boss is happy. If he is happy then I am happy. Isn't that enough?

"Did you ever read 'Brave New World' by Huxley. Some times I wish I had a 'Soma' quota at the end of the work day to carry me until the morning alarm and maybe another to get me through the day. Heck I've wondered what it would be like to go on a nice long soma holiday and just never wake up."

Reaching for his double shot of Scotch on the rocks he swigs his glass empty and plunks it on the table hard. Will shrugs and picks at a hole in the table cloth. "I don't know, maybe you're right. Maybe, I should get out more. I don't know what happened. Lately I have been peering out wondering what I am missing. Jim and Mary are heading to Cuba for a holiday in February. You and Dorothy just got back from England and here I am, year after year, just making sure my in-box is clear by the end of the day. It's been going on like this for too long and I wonder why I am addicted to old episodes of "Friends". Maybe we all have to get out of our little aquarium sooner or later, I don't know. I'm too depressed to even think about it most of the time let alone do anything about it. Will shifts his chair again.

"It's like the sun. some people chase the sun, some people are chased by the shade but some people are fortunate enough that no matte where they are the sun will creep over the dark horizon and lay across them like the lap blanket they always deserved."

More traffic rumbles by. Instead of Will raising

his voice to compete he just shuts up and settles back into his seat. The shadows of the afternoon slowly, inevitably, crawls up the side of the checkered table cloth and cross the table. Neither Will nor Frank speak for the longest time. A now cold breeze shivers them to pay their tab and move on.

The Walk Home

IT WAS A NIGHTMARE. Will Farnaby sat up and swung his legs to the side of the bed. He felt disoriented, shoulders heavy. He slumped his elbows to his knees and rubbed his eyes. The red haze that radiated from the bedside clock beamed, 3:54am. The last few minutes, or had it been hours, seemed so close to the truth of his life that he questioned why he had been on the road with his brother but there he was, clear as day, walking two paces behind him. Will muttered to himself, "How on earth did I get stuck walking home from town behind him. Him of all people?"

Will had not spoken to his brother for many years. He had skillfully orchestrated not being in the same family pictures as him, let alone in the same room. He was tired of his brother's snide, unfriendly manner. Without turning to Will his brother pivoted in his tracks, slipped on a pair of white satin gloves, picked up the handles of his wheelbarrow and started, at a quick pace, to walk. After a moment of hesitation Will grabbed his white satin gloves, grasped the handles of his wheelbarrow and hurried off to catch up.

Will had disowned his brother years ago, yet here he was trotting down the gravel road trying to catch up to him, both of them pushing wheelbarrows full of fresh, stinking horse shit. Still a few paces behind his brother he wondered what the heck he was supposed to do? Break out into song, give him a cheery back smacking "So how you doing bro?" He felt like saying "Hey you wiener, if I have to push this load of horse shit with you, you are going to tell me how you got to be such a sullen son-of-a-bitch with me. What the heck did I ever do to you to warrant pushing a wheelbarrow full of horse crap down wind from you?"

A smirk comes over Will's face with a subtle strategy. He would let his pace slow, bit by bit. He would pull back and let more and more distance fall between them. He would play a game to see if his brother would ever notice. The palpable quiet is interrupted only by the rhythmical squeaking of their wheelbarrows timed with the drumming of footfalls,

The greater the distance the greater the relief of sharing space. With consternation, Will mumbles to himself, "I have, for too many years, shared my life with him; I don't need to share another, single, breath."

With every step, Will wonders what was going through his brother's mind. His brother's normal aloof demeanor, his speechlessness is well rehearsed with years of silence under his belt. Whatever is going through his mind he walks in stoic silence, in unvaried quick pace. Will says out loud to himself, "Thank God, I am finally alone." His pace lessons until he can finally slip, out of sight, behind a tree. Even if his brother were to turn now Will would have vanished, he would not even be a footprint in the dust behind him. He would not be the squeak of a wheel or the shuffle of shoes on gravel. He simply would not be.

From Will's vantage point his brother does not turn to look where he is. His pace does not deviate. Will wonders, "is he deaf? Did he forget that I was there? Does he have no imagination whatsoever? Maybe I fell behind him and was dying in the dust." Maybe that would not matter to his brother. Never did he turn, not even once to see or say anything. His steady pace was unwavering, unyielding.

Will sat in the shade on the rim of his stinking wheelbarrow behind the tree. No brother in sight, sheltered from the penetrating sun he felt a sad, dry breeze blow the aroma of manure across the empty field.

Rubbing his eyes, slumping back into bed Will presses his head into his still hot pillow. There will be little sleep for Will tonight.

Racoon Trappin'

WILL FARNABY AND FRANK SAT in their favourite spot at Star Bucks, each leaning over a double frapacheeno. Will put down his New Yorker and leaned towards Frank.

"Frank, I've got a racoon living at my place. Damn thing keeps digging in my compost dragging sloppy stuff around making a mess. He's living in my lawnmower shed. Damn thing. Scares the crap out of me at night every time I go in the back yard. He sits there in the dark where I can't see 'im. Then all of a sudden he moves, he hisses at me and dashes off because I get too close. Gets my heart jumping every time. Damn thing.

"I guess you wouldn't happen to have a live racoon trap I can borrow? I gotta get rid of the beggar but I don't want to kill him. If I don't get rid of him he'll have babies in the spring and then I'll have a family of trouble to get rid of. That's all I need is a bunch of black-eyed bandits raiding my compost pile and digging in my little garden.

"I might have to drive out to my brother's place and see if he still has one I can borrow. He trapped one one time. He used sardines as bait – – caught a cat. Cat looked like a racoon in the dark so he left it in the trap all night and called Animal Control the next morning. It wasn't until they arrived that my brother felt damn silly. Turned out it was the neighbour's cat. He never liked the damn thing. Even though it stayed away after that. He figured it was a waste of good sardines.

"My neighbour said he used to have a live racoon trap but he threw it in the lake –– racoon was still in it. Poor beggar. I gotta get rid of my racoon. It's driving me crazy, damn thing. I actually shouldn't worry so much about it. It provides me with the only level of excitement I get these days."

Psycho Babble

THE WALL HEATER THUNDERS to life. Hot air courses into the room. A grey ceiling fan hangs motionless over Will's bed collecting dust. Morning light slivers in through drawn drapes. Will reluctantly creeps into consciousness.

Leaning forward over the bathroom sink, Will, pushes his anemic face towards the steamed mirror and rubs his hands over his morning stubble. He pulls down on his cheeks looking past his tired complection into bulging red eyes. He is oblivious to his hand written note that is stuck to the mirror. "Think Positive. You Will Make It. It's Only A Matter of Persistence." The note is curled, faded, spotted; God only knows how long it has been ignored morning after morning.

In a low grumbling voice Will pokes at his teeth and mumbles, "We are all afraid of something." Toweling steam from the mirror he sticks his tongue out as far as it will go, looks down to his tonsils and rubs his neck. He squints his eyes and says with whining cynicism, "My shrink says I'm afraid of finding out what I am afraid of. Supposedly I'm afraid of finding out just what's holding me back from being happy. It might cause change and change can be painful he says. Fear of the unknown. Hell, it all sounds like psycho babble to me."

Will squints his eyes and thinks to himself. "Will Farnaby you are pluggin' along nickle by nickle, worrying about every penny, wondering what you did to deserve this so-called sorry life that you live." He rocks his shoulders back and forth and rubs his face again. "I have three failed marriages under my belt, Rose, Mary and Ruth. My shrink says that I'm still clinging to my second ex-wife so much that I can't move more than two blocks away from her. Damn, I spent my last penny to buy Mary a lawnmower but then what did I bloody well do for fuck sakes, I also cut her grass. Why the hell didn't I just give it to her 17 year old kid to push is beyond me?" Will thumps the side of his head with the heel of his hand and roles his eyes.

With quick, agitated strokes, Will slashes at his beard with his new red Schick "race car sleek, guaranteed to make any women want to kiss his baby smooth face" razor. "My shrink says I was looking for – 'come back to me pity points'. More psycho babble if you ask me. Can't we just do something good without it having a hidden agenda. Next time I won't tell him if I do something kind and generous for my ex. I'll just tell him when I do something spiteful and mean. Next week I'll just make something up and see what he has to say about that."

Will takes a step back from the sink. Still only half-shaven he points at the mirror. "It's my job, that's what keeps me here not my ex-wives. It's my son and letting him finish his year at the same school. That's why I stick around this place, not because I want to get back with my ex-wife. Besides, it wouldn't matter, she doesn't want me anyway. I can't see that changing even if I wanted it to, which I don't." Will leans forward with hands on the cold white porcelain and looks himself straight in the eye. "Which I don't." He mumbles to himself, "I'll move back to my home town when I'm good and ready and not a minute sooner and meanwhile I'm damn proud of my job." He shrinks back down to a normal posture and almost whines. "I finally climbed two rungs up the ladder but I still always feel like I have one foot on the ground stuck in the mud. Why is the damn ladder so damn slippery?"

Leaning back from the mirror Will points back at his reflection again, "It's the system. That's what it is. You can't only have bosses, you have to have grunt workers at the bottom and lots of them. I used to be one of them. Heck I still am one. I just got a raise and a bit of respect from my boss but I'm still a ground level grunt worker wishing I could earn enough to buy a house instead of renting. What on earth am I doing wrong? All I want is a house, a garden, a car and a family to come home to after a long day of work. What I want is a wife."

Bringing the towel to his face he sniffs at it, wrinkles his nose, sniffs again and tosses it into a growing pile beside the door. Slashing at his face Will finishes shaving, splashes "Old Spice" on his face then into his arm pits and mumbles. "My damn brother wants me to move back home. My brooottthhher wants me to get half of the money out of my ex-wife's house. My brooottthhher wants me to move to his little flee bitten town, come over for dinner twice a week and live happily ever after. My brooottthhher wants... what my brother wants is for me to rent a truck and move. I can't afford to rent a damn truck let alone start looking for a job in a totally different part of the country. Will reaches for the tossed towel and dries his face.

"Afraid of success, my shrink said, or was that afraid of failure? I still don't understand the bloody difference. It's just more psycho babble to me. How about afraid of not paying my rent? I bounced my rent cheque last month because I was five bucks short. Now that's not psycho babble.

"Holy crap look at the time. I had better get in

gear. Maybe if I stopped going to the damn shrink I could afford to rent a truck and move. Maybe after the school year is done." Will jots down a note on a scrap, envelope from the garbage and places it on the table just before he slams the door behind himself - Don't forget to take out Rose's garbage tonight.

Cold Steel

SITTING ON THE SIDE OF HIS BED, Will Farnaby slumps and stares at a new hole in his sock. His untrimmed big toenail has scissored its way into open air. "I'm fuckin' pathetic," he says out loud to himself. "You aren't even motivated enough to cut your own damn toenails let alone get another job or get rid of the damn racoon in the back yard. Maybe your shrink isn't as stupid as you think. Stupid idiot, you deserve every bit of crap that comes your way." Wiggling his toe he leans over, yanks the sock off of his foot and apathetically throughs it across the room at an unruly pile of dirty laundry.

This was the last straw. In that instant Will plummeted from depression into the dark depths of hopelessness. He was now more despondent than he thought possible. Three times divorced, stuck in a boring, unsatisfying job and now a hole in his sock. Will had slowly, one by one, let friends and social activities drain from his life. The only real friend he had left was Frank but even Frank now had Dorothy.

Self-pity grew to be his only companion. It

grew in Will like black mould in a petri dish, smothering, eventually filling every crevice of his life. It felt to Will like life was just not worth living. His discontent was more than the general malaise that had hovered in his life for years. It was now the constant unyielding consternation of self-deprecation. At this moment it seemed there was only one way out.

    Will reached for the revolver that had been sitting conspicuously on his night table for weeks and jammes the cold muzzle into his mouth. Pointing the barrel to the roof of his mouth he pulls gingerly on the trigger and stops. He toggles the hammer back and forth ever so gently. He wondered just how far he could pull the trigger before the gun would fire and it would all be over. He wondered if anyone would care. Will gently releases the trigger. With muzzle still in his mouth he whips tears from his eyes and again pulls gently, just a little further this time and again gently releases. Pulling the barrel from his mouth he throughs the gun violently across the room smashing a lamp before it comes to rest in the corner.

    With a calm sense of resignation Will reaches for a pen and pauses over the note pad that he pulls from a stack of papers and books on his night table.

Dear Mary: I have to take care of this one last thing before I leave. I have to apologize for being such a jerk. I have finally come to a painful realization of just how utterly selfish I am. When I was over at your place last week I took the last slice of the special raisin bread that you like so much. Even though I jokingly offered it around to others with my mock auction – "Going once, going twice, going... too late it's mine." I should not have taken the last piece. Even though I beat myself up over this I realized that I never apologized to you. I can't help it, I tell myself over and over again that it does not have to be me, me, me – I am sorry. It seems that I will never learn – I will never learn. I am sorry. Will Farnaby.

    With precision Will slowly tares the paper from the pad and with gentle care folds it into quarters. Pressing his hand across the final fold he stands the tented paper like a card on the night table where the gun once sat.
    Shuffling to the corner of the room, Will, kicks the broken lamp out of his way, picks up the flung revolver and sticks the cold steel muzzle back in his mouth. Penetrating the barrel with the tip of he tongue he is shocked by the acidic chemical residue. Sucking air through the barrel he slowly, ever so slowly, with deliberate hesitation pulls the trigger. This time all the way.

The End!

Biographical Sketch of Author:

Richard M. Grove was born into an artist family in Hamilton, Ontario, on October 7, 1953. With both parents artists and gallery owners he had a unique and early introduction into the world of visual art. His first experience with art was with photography when at the age of thirteen he purchased, with his father's enthusiasm and help, his first single lens reflex camera. Over the ensuing years, after leaving high school, he studied pottery at Mohawk College, design and pottery at Sheridan College, leading to his graduating in 1984 from the Experimental Arts Department at Ontario College of Art. In 1994 he graduated with honours from the Humber College, Arts Administration diploma course. In 2002 he returned to school to study computer courses relating to publishing.

Since graduating from Ontario College of Art, Richard has exhibited in more than twenty, solo and group exhibitions in Hamilton, Toronto, Boston, Calgary and Grand Prairie. He has his art in over thirty corporate collections across Canada, the most prominent of which are Esso Resources, Continental Insurance, Alberta Energy Corporation and Calgary District Hospital Group. These four companies alone represent a collection of almost thirty pieces of his work.

Among the many corporate collections are six commissions of different styles and mediums ranging from pastel on paper to acrylic on canvas.

His photography and digital paintings have been on the cover of numerous books and periodicals. His book of digital paintings and poetry entitled "Sky Over Presqu'ile" was published in 2003, "Substantiality" a book of digital paintings was published in 2006 with a book of photography entitled "Oxido Rojo" released in the fall of 2006 followed by a book of Photography entitled "terra firma".

Along with his visual art, Richard has been writing poetry seriously for decades and has had over 100 of his poems published in periodicals and has been published in over 25 anthologies from around the world. Including his poetry and photography he has 10 titles to his name. To mention only two of his poetry titles, his book entitled "Beyond Fear and Anger" was released in 1997 and his book published by Micro Prose, entitled "Poems For Jack" was released in 2002. He is also the author of numerous books with metaphysical themes including "The Mind–Body Connection", "Metaphysical Healing For a Secular Age" and "A Spiritual Study of Body". You can reach him at writers@hiddenbrookpress.com.

He is an editor and publisher and runs a growing publishing company Hidden Brook Press from which he publishes poetry contest anthologies and books of every genre for authors around the world. Aside from being a published poet, Richard has also exhibited his poetry in acrylic on paper paintings as well as in audio sculptures. For his poetry and prose, Richard has won a few small prizes and honourable mentions as well as a finalist spot in two contest anthologies. For his short stories he has won a top ten prize.

Richard is the founder of the Canadian Poet Registry, an archival information website that lists Canadian poets including: biographical information, their book titles and awards. One can view this website at - http://www.hiddenbrookpress.com/Registry.htm. He was an active member of the Canadian Poetry Association for ten years serving on the executive for seven years including five as President. He is the founding president of both the CCLA (2004) – Canada Cuba Literary Alliance - www.CanadaCuba LiteraryAlliance.org and the CCLA Federation of Photographers (2006). The CCLA has an international membership and boasts a full-colour literary journal called The Ambassador and a literary e-newsletter called The Envoy. He is the founding president of the Brighton Arts Council and the co-founder of the Purdy Country Literary Festival.

Richard has also been a public speaker MCing poetry readings and other literary events. He has been invited by a number of literary groups as Feature Speaker on various topics in Cuba, Germany, USA, New Zealand and Canada. He was also the Feature Author as publisher/poet in the October 1998 issue of "The Treasure Chest" published out of Virginia, USA and Feature Poet in "Poetry Canada" in 2004.

Richard now lives with his wife, Kim, a writer, editor and teacher, in Presqu'ile Provincial Park situated halfway between Toronto and Kingston, south of the 401 hwy. Their location is a constant inspiration for their work.

Books by Richard M. Grove

- Beyond Fear and Anger
- Poems For Jack: Poems for the Poetically Challenged
- A View of Contrasts: Cuba Poems
- The Mind Body Connection
- Sky Over Presqu'ile
- terra firma
- Oxido Rojo
- Substantiality
- A Spiritual Study of Body
- The Family Reunion
- From Cross Hill: Views of My Cuba
- Psycho Babble and the Consternations of Life
- a trip to banes, Cuba, 2002
- Trapped In Paradise – Views of My Cuba

Author's Notes:

— Will Farnaby – is the main character in Aldous Huxley's novel "Island". My Will Farnaby has an antethetical life experience from Huxley's Will Farnaby

— Soma – The mind altering drug in Aldous Huxley's novel "Brave New World". Soma is used to escape reality.

— Soma Holiday – A citizen in Aldous Huxley's novel "Brave New World" would take Soma for an extended length of time as a holiday. They would die if they took the drug for too long of a period.

— Koi – A large Japanees goldfish type of fish often seen in ponds or large restaurant aquariums.

— Friends – A situation comedy from television in the late 1900s.

Previoiusly Published:

Psycho Babble – previously published in The Envoy - issue 008 – 2006

Antonio's Only Resting Place – previously published in "Shores of Time" CCLA